DON'T CALL ME FATSO

by Barbara Philips

illustrated by Helen Cogancherry

Chariot Books
DAVID C. COOK PUBLISHING CO.

ita and Sue plopped down at a table in the school cafeteria.

Rita opened her lunch box. In no time at all, she finished her peanut butter and jelly sandwich, her marshmallow creme cookies, and her chocolate milk. Then she wrinkled her nose.

"I *told* Mom I hate carrot sticks," she said. "Hey, Sue, I'll trade you my carrots for your cookies."

"Are you blind?" asked Sue. "I just ate some carrots. Anyway, I don't have cookies. My mother gave me a pear instead."

"Well, let's hurry up," said Rita. "It's almost time to go back."

5

Their teacher, Ms. O'Leary, was waiting for them in the hall.

"Everyone get in line," she said. "We're going to see the school nurse."

Rita walked along with the others to the nurse's office.

"It's time for you all to be weighed and measured," the nurse told them. "We'll do this again from time to time, so we can tell how much you're growing."

Everyone took turns standing on the scale. Soon it was Rita's turn.

She heard someone whisper behind her: "Let's see if Fatso breaks the scale!"

"Be quiet, Allen," Ms. O'Leary warned.

Don't call me Fatso! Rita wanted to shout. But she was too shy to say it out loud.

Then the nurse said, "Seventy-five pounds." He bent down to Rita. "Let's see what your weight is next time. We might want to think about a diet for you."

Rita had already stopped listening. She was the heaviest person in class!

9

On the way back to the classroom, Rita
pretended to be invisible. *At least the next
class will make me feel better*, she thought. It
was her favorite class, art, with her favorite
teacher, Mr. Simpson.

"I want everyone to move your chairs into a big circle," said Mr. Simpson. "Then start drawing a picture of someone in class."

Rita got right to work on a picture of Sue. She didn't even look up when she heard some boys snickering in the corner.

Mr. Simpson walked over to Allen and Mick. "Are you boys finished?" he asked.

They nodded their heads, still laughing.

"We drew Rita," said Mick.

"You mean Fatso," Allen said.

Then they held up their pictures. On each paper were two large circles, with tiny dots for eyes and mouth.

"Don't ever do this again," Mr. Simpson scolded. "People come in all shapes and sizes, and that's no reason to make fun of them."

Rita just looked down at her drawing.

13

That night, Rita helped her stepfather with the supper dishes. She was very quiet. "Something wrong?" he asked her.

'Dad, the nurse weighed us today. I'm the heaviest in my class!" she cried. "The boys call me names. Nobody likes a fatso."

"Kids always make fun of something," Dad said. "When I was your age, everyone laughed at my big ears. But it's what's inside you that really counts. *We* love you just the way you are."

"I like your ears," said Rita. "What I don't like is being fat."

"Come to think of it, I could stand to lose some weight too. Why don't we do something about it?"

"You mean a diet?" Rita asked.

"Sort of," he answered. "We could stop eating sweet things and drinking soda pop. And let's stop having desserts all the time. If we're still hungry after dinner, we'll have an apple."

"An apple? But cake tastes much better!"

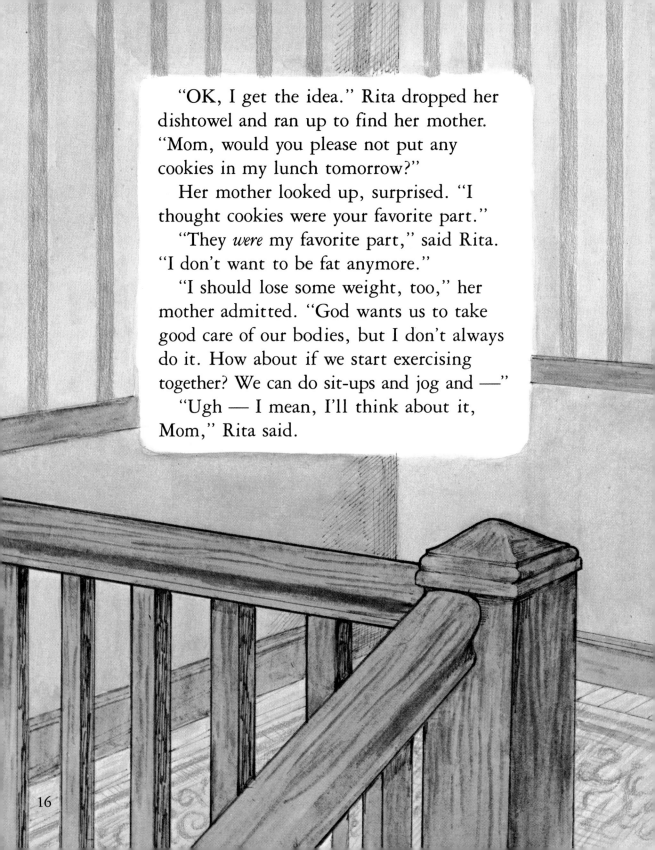

"OK, I get the idea." Rita dropped her dishtowel and ran up to find her mother. "Mom, would you please not put any cookies in my lunch tomorrow?"

Her mother looked up, surprised. "I thought cookies were your favorite part."

"They *were* my favorite part," said Rita. "I don't want to be fat anymore."

"I should lose some weight, too," her mother admitted. "God wants us to take good care of our bodies, but I don't always do it. How about if we start exercising together? We can do sit-ups and jog and —"

"Ugh — I mean, I'll think about it, Mom," Rita said.

The next morning, Sue and Rita walked to school together. *Sue's a real friend,* Rita thought. *She likes me just the way I am.*

"I'm going to take swimming lessons on Saturday mornings," Sue said. "Want to come?"

Rita started to say no. She liked to
spend Saturday mornings watching TV.
Then she changed her mind.

"Swimming is good exercise, right?
Well, I'd rather swim than jog!"

Rita hated swimming lessons at first.
Putting her head underwater never seemed
like a very good idea.

After a few lessons, she began having more fun.

The day came when she was able to swim all the way across the pool.

"You're quite a swimmer!" called the teacher.

Rita beamed. After that, she could hardly wait for each Saturday morning to come.

One morning the swimming teacher told the class, "Today we're going to jump off the diving board and swim to the other side."

Rita gulped. She was still a little afraid of deep water. When her turn came to jump, she stood on the diving board for a long time.

"Hurry, please," said the teacher. "We don't have all day."

Rita shut her eyes and jumped.

Splash! It felt like half the water in the pool was going up Rita's nose! Coughing and choking, she barely made it to the other side.

As she dragged herself out of the pool, Rita overheard someone whispering, "She's so fat that she sinks when she dives!"

That day Rita bought three candy bars on her way home from swimming. She was finishing the last one by the time she walked in the door.

Rita's stepfather saw the candy wrappers in her hand. "What's this?" he asked. "I thought you quit eating sweets."

"Oh, who cares!" cried Rita. "I went on a diet, but it didn't do any good. I'm still fat, and the kids still laugh at me."

"Losing weight takes time, just like learning to swim does."

"But it's already been a long time!"

"I know," he said. "And that's just why you shouldn't quit now — just because things seem hard. You'll feel better about yourself if you keep up the good work."

Rita decided to keep trying. When her friends had ice cream, she had an apple. When they had potato chips and soda, she had celery sticks and orange juice. One day, when Allen called her Fatso, she asked him to stop calling her that.

On the last day of swimming lessons, the teacher spoke to Rita. "You're almost ready for the advanced class. But before I pass you, I have to see you jump off that diving board."

Rita felt sick. Her heart pounded madly as she walked to the end of the board.

I just have to pass, she told herself. *I don't want to stay with the beginners all my life.*

"One, two, three, go!" the teacher counted.

Rita jumped. Without even thinking about it, suddenly she was swimming across the pool.

"You did it," cheered the teacher. "Good for you!"

And swimming *was* good for her, Rita realized. She kept on taking lessons, and as time went by, she stopped missing sweets so much.

One night at dinner, her stepfather read a Bible verse: "Honor God with your bodies." Then he thanked Rita for helping to improve the health habits of the whole family.

Then came the day that Rita's class went back to the school nurse.

Oh, I hope I've lost weight, Rita sighed to herself. *I never want to be called Fatso again.*

When Rita stepped on the scale, the nurse called out, "Seventy pounds."

Rita almost fell off the scale. "You mean I only lost *five pounds?*" she asked.

The nurse looked at the chart. "But look," he said. "Since the last time I saw you, you've grown more than an inch. You're just fine."

"You really think so?"

"You're as healthy as can be," he told her. "A growing girl shouldn't lose too much weight."

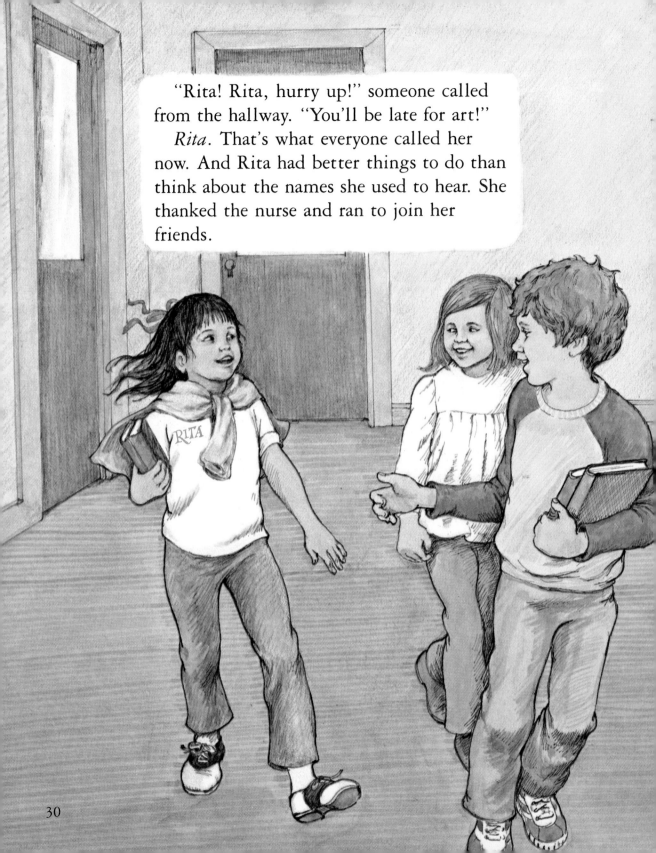

"Rita! Rita, hurry up!" someone called from the hallway. "You'll be late for art!"

Rita. That's what everyone called her now. And Rita had better things to do than think about the names she used to hear. She thanked the nurse and ran to join her friends.